ARIEL

BOOKS BY SYLVIA PLATH

The Colossus (1960)

Ariel (1965)

Crossing the Water (1971)

Winter Trees (1971)

The Bell Jar (1971)

The Collected Poems (1981)

sylvia plath

ARIEL

PERENNIAL CLASSICS

HarperCollins books may be purchased for educational, business, or sales promotional use. For information please write: Special Markets Department, HarperCollins Publishers, Inc., 10 East 53rd Street, New York, NY 10022.

First PERENNIAL LIBRARY edition published 1975.

First Perennial Classics edition published 1999.
Perennial Classics are published by HarperPerennial, a division of HarperCollins Publishers.

Library of Congress Cataloging-in-Publication Data
Plath, Sylvia.
    Ariel / Sylvia Plath. — 1st Perennial Classics ed.
    p. cm.
    ISBN 0-06-093172-8
    I. Title.
PS3566.L27A7 1999
811'.54–dc21   98-56144

03 ❖/RRD-H 20 19 18 17 16 15 14 13 12 11

For
FRIEDA *and* NICHOLAS

Acknowledgments

ॐ

The poems *Tulips*, *The Elm Speaks* (appearing in this book as *Elm*) and *The Moon and the Yew Tree* appeared originally in *The New Yorker*.

Fever 103° originally appeared in *Poetry Magazine*.

A Birthday Present was originally published in *Critical Quarterly*—England.

Other poems in this book appeared in *The Atlantic Monthly*, *Encounter*, *Harper's Magazine*, *London Magazine*, the *New York Review of Books*, and *The Observer*.

Contents

༄

FOREWORD by Robert Lowell   xiii

MORNING SONG   1

THE COURIERS   2

SHEEP IN FOG   3

THE APPLICANT   4

LADY LAZARUS   6

TULIPS   10

CUT   13

ELM   15

THE NIGHT DANCES   18

POPPIES IN OCTOBER   20

BERCK-PLAGE   21

ARIEL   29

DEATH & CO.   31

LESBOS   33

NICK AND THE CANDLESTICK   37

GULLIVER 39

GETTING THERE 41

MEDUSA 44

THE MOON AND THE YEW TREE 46

A BIRTHDAY PRESENT 48

MARY'S SONG 52

LETTER IN NOVEMBER 53

THE RIVAL 55

DADDY 56

YOU'RE 60

FEVER 103° 61

THE BEE MEETING 64

THE ARRIVAL OF THE BEE BOX 67

STINGS 69

THE SWARM 72

WINTERING 75

THE HANGING MAN 77

LITTLE FUGUE 78

YEARS 81

THE MUNICH MANNEQUINS 82

TOTEM 84

PARALYTIC 86

BALLOONS   88

POPPIES IN JULY   90

KINDNESS   91

CONTUSION   92

EDGE   93

WORDS   95

About Sylvia Plath   97

Foreword

❧

In these poems, written in the last months of her life and often rushed out at the rate of two or three a day, Sylvia Plath becomes herself, becomes something imaginary, newly, wildly and subtly created—hardly a person at all, or a woman, certainly not another "poetess," but one of those super-real, hypnotic, great classical heroines. This character is feminine, rather than female, though almost everything we customarily think of as feminine is turned on its head. The voice is now coolly amused, witty, now sour, now fanciful, girlish, charming, now sinking to the strident rasp of the vampire—a Dido, Phaedra, or Medea, who can laugh at herself as "cow-heavy and floral in my Victorian nightgown." Though lines get repeated, and sometimes the plot is lost, language never dies in her mouth.

Everything in these poems is personal, confessional, felt, but the manner of feeling is controlled hallucination, the autobiography of a fever. She burns to be on the move, a walk, a ride, a journey, the flight of the queen bee. She is driven forward by the pounding pistons of her heart. The title *Ariel* summons up Shakespeare's lovely, though slightly chilling and androgenous spirit, but the truth is that this *Ariel* is the author's horse. Dangerous, more powerful than man, machinelike from hard training, she herself is a little like a racehorse, galloping relentlessly with risked, outstretched neck, death hurdle after death hurdle topped. She cries out for that rapid life of starting pistols, snapping tapes, and new world records broken. What is most heroic in her, though, is not her force, but the desperate practicality of her control, her hand of metal with its modest, womanish touch. Almost pure motion, she can endure "God, the great stasis in his vacuous night," hospitals, fever, paralysis, the iron lung, being stripped like a girl in the booth of a circus sideshow, dressed like a mannequin, tied down like Gulliver by the Lilliputians . . . apartments, babies, prim English landscapes, beehives, yew trees, gardens, the moon, hooks, the black boot, wounds, flowers with mouths like wounds, Belsen's lampshades made of human skin, Hitler's homicidal iron tanks clanking over Russia. Suicide, father-hatred, self-loathing—nothing is too much for the macabre gaiety of her control. Yet it is too much; her art's immortality is life's disintegration. The surprise, the shimmering, unwrapped birthday present, the transcendence "into the red eye, the cauldron of morning," and the lover, who are always waiting for her, are Death, her own abrupt and defiant death.

> *He tells me how badly I photograph.*
> *He tells me how sweet*
> *The babies look in their hospital*
> *Icebox, a simple*

Frill at the neck,
Then the flutings of their Ionian
Death-gowns,
Then two little feet.

There is a peculiar, haunting challenge to these poems. Probably many, after reading *Ariel*, will recoil from their first overawed shock, and painfully wonder why so much of it leaves them feeling empty, evasive and inarticulate. In her lines, I often hear the serpent whisper, "Come, if only you had the courage, you too could have my rightness, audacity and ease of inspiration." But most of us will turn back. These poems are playing Russian roulette with six cartridges in the cylinder, a game of "chicken," the wheels of both cars locked and unable to swerve. Oh, for that heaven of the humble copyist, those millennia of Egyptian artists repeating their lofty set patterns! And yet Sylvia Plath's poems are not the celebration of some savage and debauched existence, that of the "damned" poet, glad to burn out his body for a few years of continuous intensity. This poetry and life are not a career; they tell that life, even when disciplined, is simply not worth it.

It is poignant, looking back, to realize that the secret of Sylvia Plath's last irresistible blaze lies lost somewhere in the checks and courtesies of her early laborious shyness. She was never a student of mine, but for a couple of months seven years ago, she used to drop in on my poetry seminar at Boston University. I see her dim against the bright sky of a high window, viewless unless one cared to look down on the city outskirts' defeated yellow brick and square concrete pillbox filling stations. She was willowy, long-waisted, sharp-elbowed, nervous, giggly, gracious—a brilliant tense presence embarrassed by restraint. Her humility and willingness to accept what was admired seemed at times to give her an air of maddening docility that hid her unfashionable patience and boldness. She showed us poems that later, more or less unchanged, went into her first book, *The Colossus*. They were somber, formidably expert in stanza structure, and had a flair for alliteration and Massachusetts' low-tide dolor.

> *A mongrel working his legs to a gallop*
> *Hustles the gull flock to flap off the sand-spit.*

Other lines showed her wit and directness.

> *The pears fatten like little Buddhas.*

Somehow none of it sank very deep into my awareness. I sensed her abashment and distinction, and never guessed her later appalling and triumphant fulfillment.

ROBERT LOWELL
NEW YORK CITY
1966

ARIEL

Morning Song

Love set you going like a fat gold watch.
The midwife slapped your footsoles, and your bald cry
Took its place among the elements.

Our voices echo, magnifying your arrival. New statue.
In a drafty museum, your nakedness
Shadows our safety. We stand round blankly as walls.

I'm no more your mother
Than the cloud that distils a mirror to reflect its own slow
Effacement at the wind's hand.

All night your moth-breath
Flickers among the flat pink roses. I wake to listen:
A far sea moves in my ear.

One cry, and I stumble from bed, cow-heavy and floral
In my Victorian nightgown.
Your mouth opens clean as a cat's. The window square

Whitens and swallows its dull stars. And now you try
Your handful of notes;
The clear vowels rise like balloons.

The Couriers

❧

The word of a snail on the plate of a leaf?
It is not mine. Do not accept it.

Acetic acid in a sealed tin?
Do not accept it. It is not genuine.

A ring of gold with the sun in it?
Lies. Lies and a grief.

Frost on a leaf, the immaculate
Cauldron, talking and crackling

All to itself on the top of each
Of nine black Alps.

A disturbance in mirrors,
The sea shattering its grey one——

Love, love, my season.

Sheep in Fog

The hills step off into whiteness.
People or stars
Regard me sadly, I disappoint them.

The train leaves a line of breath.
O slow
Horse the colour of rust,

Hooves, dolorous bells——
All morning the
Morning has been blackening,

A flower left out.
My bones hold a stillness, the far
Fields melt my heart.

They threaten
To let me through to a heaven
Starless and fatherless, a dark water.

The Applicant

First, are you our sort of a person?
Do you wear
A glass eye, false teeth or a crutch,
A brace or a hook,
Rubber breasts or a rubber crotch,

Stitches to show something's missing? No, no? Then
How can we give you a thing?
Stop crying.
Open your hand.
Empty? Empty. Here is a hand

To fill it and willing
To bring teacups and roll away headaches
And do whatever you tell it.
Will you marry it?
It is guaranteed

To thumb shut your eyes at the end
And dissolve of sorrow.
We make new stock from the salt.
I notice you are stark naked.
How about this suit——

Black and stiff, but not a bad fit.
Will you marry it?

It is waterproof, shatterproof, proof
Against fire and bombs through the roof.
Believe me, they'll bury you in it.

Now your head, excuse me, is empty.
I have the ticket for that.
Come here, sweetie, out of the closet.
Well, what do you think of *that*?
Naked as paper to start

But in twenty-five years she'll be silver,
In fifty, gold.
A living doll, everywhere you look.
It can sew, it can cook,
It can talk, talk, talk.

It works, there is nothing wrong with it.
You have a hole, it's a poultice.
You have an eye, it's an image.
My boy, it's your last resort.
Will you marry it, marry it, marry it.

Lady Lazarus

I have done it again.
One year in every ten
I manage it——

A sort of walking miracle, my skin
Bright as a Nazi lampshade,
My right foot

A paperweight,
My face a featureless, fine
Jew linen.

Peel off the napkin
O my enemy.
Do I terrify?——

The nose, the eye pits, the full set of teeth?
The sour breath
Will vanish in a day.

Soon, soon the flesh
The grave cave ate will be
At home on me

And I a smiling woman.
I am only thirty.
And like a cat I have nine times to die.

This is Number Three.
What a trash
To annihilate each decade.

What a million filaments.
The peanut-crunching crowd
Shoves in to see

Them unwrap me hand and foot——
The big strip tease.
Gentlemen, ladies,

These are my hands,
My knees.
I may be skin and bone,

Nevertheless, I am the same, identical woman.
The first time it happened I was ten.
It was an accident.

The second time I meant
To last it out and not come back at all.
I rocked shut

As a seashell.
They had to call and call
And pick the worms off me like sticky pearls.

Dying
Is an art, like everything else.
I do it exceptionally well.

I do it so it feels like hell.
I do it so it feels real.
I guess you could say I've a call.

It's easy enough to do it in a cell.
It's easy enough to do it and stay put.
It's the theatrical

Comeback in broad day
To the same place, the same face, the same brute
Amused shout:

"A miracle!"
That knocks me out.
There is a charge

For the eyeing of my scars, there is a charge
For the hearing of my heart——
It really goes.

And there is a charge, a very large charge,
For a word or a touch
Or a bit of blood

Or a piece of my hair or my clothes.
So, so, Herr Doktor.
So, Herr Enemy.

I am your opus,
I am your valuable,
The pure gold baby

That melts to a shriek.
I turn and burn.
Do not think I underestimate your great concern.

Ash, ash—
You poke and stir.
Flesh, bone, there is nothing there——

A cake of soap.
A wedding ring,
A gold filling.

Herr God, Herr Lucifer,
Beware
Beware.

Out of the ash
I rise with my red hair
And I eat men like air.

Tulips

The tulips are too excitable, it is winter here.
Look how white everything is, how quiet, how snowed-in.
I am learning peacefulness, lying by myself quietly
As the light lies on these white walls, this bed, these hands.
I am nobody; I have nothing to do with explosions.
I have given my name and my day-clothes up to the nurses
And my history to the anaesthetist and my body to surgeons.

They have propped my head between the pillow and the
    sheet-cuff
Like an eye between two white lids that will not shut.
Stupid pupil, it has to take everything in.
The nurses pass and pass, they are no trouble,
They pass the way gulls pass inland in their white caps,
Doing things with their hands, one just the same as another,
So it is impossible to tell how many there are.

My body is a pebble to them, they tend it as water
Tends to the pebbles it must run over, smoothing them gently.
They bring me numbness in their bright needles, they bring
    me sleep.
Now I have lost myself I am sick of baggage——
My patent leather overnight case like a black pillbox,
My husband and child smiling out of the family photo;
Their smiles catch onto my skin, little smiling hooks.

I have let things slip, a thirty-year-old cargo boat
Stubbornly hanging on to my name and address.

They have swabbed me clear of my loving associations.
Scared and bare on the green plastic-pillowed trolley
I watched my tea-set, my bureaus of linen, my books
Sink out of sight, and the water went over my head.
I am a nun now, I have never been so pure.

I didn't want any flowers, I only wanted
To lie with my hands turned up and be utterly empty.
How free it is, you have no idea how free——
The peacefulness is so big it dazes you,
And it asks nothing, a name tag, a few trinkets.
It is what the dead close on, finally; I imagine them
Shutting their mouths on it, like a Communion tablet.

The tulips are too red in the first place, they hurt me.
Even through the gift paper I could hear them breathe
Lightly, through their white swaddlings, like an awful baby.
Their redness talks to my wound, it corresponds.
They are subtle: they seem to float, though they weigh me
     down,
Upsetting me with their sudden tongues and their colour,
A dozen red lead sinkers round my neck.

Nobody watched me before, now I am watched.
The tulips turn to me, and the window behind me
Where once a day the light slowly widens and slowly thins,
And I see myself, flat, ridiculous, a cut-paper shadow
Between the eye of the sun and the eyes of the tulips,
And I have no face, I have wanted to efface myself.
The vivid tulips eat my oxygen.

Before they came the air was calm enough,
Coming and going, breath by breath, without any fuss.
Then the tulips filled it up like a loud noise.
Now the air snags and eddies round them the way a river
Snags and eddies round a sunken rust-red engine.
They concentrate my attention, that was happy
Playing and resting without committing itself.

The walls, also, seem to be warming themselves.
The tulips should be behind bars like dangerous animals;
They are opening like the mouth of some great African cat,
And I am aware of my heart: it opens and closes
Its bowl of red blooms out of sheer love of me.
The water I taste is warm and salt, like the sea,
And comes from a country far away as health.

Cut

For Susan O'Neill Roe

What a thrill——
My thumb instead of an onion.
The top quite gone
Except for a sort of a hinge

Of skin,
A flap like a hat,
Dead white.
Then that red plush.

Little pilgrim,
The Indian's axed your scalp.
Your turkey wattle
Carpet rolls

Straight from the heart.
I step on it,
Clutching my bottle
Of pink fizz.

A celebration, this is.
Out of a gap
A million soldiers run,
Redcoats, every one.

Whose side are they on?
O my
Homunculus, I am ill.
I have taken a pill to kill

The thin
Papery feeling.
Saboteur,
Kamikaze man——

The stain on your
Gauze Ku Klux Klan
Babushka
Darkens and tarnishes and when

The balled
Pulp of your heart
Confronts its small
Mill of silence

How you jump——
Trepanned veteran,
Dirty girl,
Thumb stump.

Elm

For Ruth Fainlight

I know the bottom, she says. I know it with my great tap root:
It is what you fear.
I do not fear it: I have been there.

Is it the sea you hear in me,
Its dissatisfactions?
Or the voice of nothing, that was your madness?

Love is a shadow.
How you lie and cry after it.
Listen: these are its hooves: it has gone off, like a horse.

All night I shall gallop thus, impetuously,
Till your head is a stone, your pillow a little turf,
Echoing, echoing.

Or shall I bring you the sound of poisons?
This is rain now, this big hush.
And this is the fruit of it: tin-white, like arsenic.

I have suffered the atrocity of sunsets.
Scorched to the root
My red filaments burn and stand, a hand of wires.

Now I break up in pieces that fly about like clubs.
A wind of such violence
Will tolerate no bystanding: I must shriek.

The moon, also, is merciless: she would drag me
Cruelly, being barren.
Her radiance scathes me. Or perhaps I have caught her.

I let her go. I let her go
Diminished and flat, as after radical surgery.
How your bad dreams possess and endow me.

I am inhabited by a cry.
Nightly it flaps out
Looking, with its hooks, for something to love.

I am terrified by this dark thing
That sleeps in me;
All day I feel its soft, feathery turnings, its malignity.

Clouds pass and disperse.
Are those the faces of love, those pale irretrievables?
Is it for such I agitate my heart?

I am incapable of more knowledge.
What is this, this face
So murderous in its strangle of branches?——

Its snaky acids kiss.
It petrifies the will. These are the isolate, slow faults
That kill, that kill, that kill.

The Night Dances
❧

A smile fell in the grass.
Irretrievable!

And how will your night dances
Lose themselves. In mathematics?

Such pure leaps and spirals——
Surely they travel

The world forever, I shall not entirely
Sit emptied of beauties, the gift

Of your small breath, the drenched grass
Smell of your sleeps, lilies, lilies.

Their flesh bears no relation.
Cold folds of ego, the calla,

And the tiger, embellishing itself——
Spots, and a spread of hot petals.

The comets
Have such a space to cross,

Such coldness, forgetfulness.
So your gestures flake off——

Warm and human, then their pink light
Bleeding and peeling

Through the black amnesias of heaven.
Why am I given

These lamps, these planets
Falling like blessings, like flakes

Six-sided, white
On my eyes, my lips, my hair

Touching and melting.
Nowhere.

Poppies in October

Even the sun-clouds this morning cannot manage such skirts.
Nor the woman in the ambulance
Whose red heart blooms through her coat so astoundingly——

A gift, a love gift
Utterly unasked for
By a sky

Palely and flamily
Igniting its carbon monoxides, by eyes
Dulled to a halt under bowlers.

O my God, what am I
That these late mouths should cry open
In a forest of frost, in a dawn of cornflowers.

Berck-Plage

❧

(I)

This is the sea, then, this great abeyance.
How the sun's poultice draws on my inflammation.

Electrifyingly-coloured sherbets, scooped from the freeze
By pale girls, travel the air in scorched hands.

Why is it so quiet, what are they hiding?
I have two legs, and I move smilingly.

A sandy damper kills the vibrations;
It stretches for miles, the shrunk voices

Waving and crutchless, half their old size.
The lines of the eye, scalded by these bald surfaces,

Boomerang like anchored elastics, hurting the owner.
Is it any wonder he puts on dark glasses?

Is it any wonder he affects a black cassock?
Here he comes now, among the mackerel gatherers

Who wall up their backs against him.
They are handling the black and green lozenges like the parts
    of a body.

The sea, that crystallized these,
Creeps away, many-snaked, with a long hiss of distress.

(II)

This black boot has no mercy for anybody.
Why should it, it is the hearse of a dead foot,

The high, dead, toeless foot of this priest
Who plumbs the well of his book,

The bent print bulging before him like scenery.
Obscene bikinis hide in the dunes,

Breasts and hips a confectioner's sugar
Of little crystals, titillating the light,

While a green pool opens its eye,
Sick with what it has swallowed——

Limbs, images, shrieks. Behind the concrete bunkers
Two lovers unstick themselves.

O white sea-crockery,
What cupped sighs, what salt in the throat. . . .

And the onlooker, trembling,
Drawn like a long material

Through a still virulence,
And a weed, hairy as privates.

(III)

On the balconies of the hotel, things are glittering.
Things, things——

Tubular steel wheelchairs, aluminium crutches.
Such salt-sweetness. Why should I walk

Beyond the breakwater, spotty with barnacles?
I am not a nurse, white and attendant,

I am not a smile.
These children are after something, with hooks and cries,

And my heart too small to bandage their terrible faults.
This is the side of a man: his red ribs,

The nerves bursting like trees, and this is the surgeon:
One mirrory eye——

A facet of knowledge.
On a striped mattress in one room

An old man is vanishing.
There is no help in his weeping wife.

Where are the eye-stones, yellow and valuable,
And the tongue, sapphire of ash.

(IV)

A wedding-cake face in a paper frill.
How superior he is now.

It is like possessing a saint.
The nurses in their wing-caps are no longer so beautiful;

They are browning, like touched gardenias.
The bed is rolled from the wall.

This is what it is to be complete. It is horrible.
Is he wearing pajamas or an evening suit

Under the glued sheet from which his powdery beak
Rises so whitely unbuffeted?

They propped his jaw with a book until it stiffened
And folded his hands, that were shaking: goodbye, goodbye.

Now the washed sheets fly in the sun,
The pillow cases are sweetening.

It is a blessing, it is a blessing:
The long coffin of soap-coloured oak,

The curious bearers and the raw date
Engraving itself in silver with marvellous calm.

(V)

The grey sky lowers, the hills like a green sea
Run fold upon fold far off, concealing their hollows,

The hollows in which rock the thoughts of the wife——
Blunt, practical boats

Full of dresses and hats and china and married daughters.
In the parlour of the stone house

One curtain is flickering from the open window,
Flickering and pouring, a pitiful candle.

This is the tongue of the dead man: remember, remember.
How far he is now, his actions

Around him like livingroom furniture, like a décor.
As the pallors gather——

The pallors of hands and neighbourly faces,
The elate pallors of flying iris.

They are flying off into nothing: remember us.
The empty benches of memory look over stones,

Marble façades with blue veins, and jelly-glassfuls of daffodils.
It is so beautiful up here: it is a stopping place.

(VI)

The natural fatness of these lime leaves!——
Pollarded green balls, the trees march to church.

The voice of the priest, in thin air,
Meets the corpse at the gate,

Addressing it, while the hills roll the notes of the dead bell;
A glitter of wheat and crude earth.

What is the name of that colour?——
Old blood of caked walls the sun heals,

Old blood of limb stumps, burnt hearts.
The widow with her black pocketbook and three daughters,

Necessary among the flowers,
Enfolds her face like fine linen,

Not to be spread again.
While a sky, wormy with put-by smiles,

Passes cloud after cloud.
And the bride flowers expend a freshness,

And the soul is a bride
In a still place, and the groom is red and forgetful, he is
   featureless.

(VII)

Behind the glass of this car
The world purrs, shut-off and gentle.

And I am dark-suited and still, a member of the party,
Gliding up in low gear behind the cart.

And the priest is a vessel,
A tarred fabric, sorry and dull,

Following the coffin on its flowery cart like a beautiful woman,
A crest of breasts, eyelids and lips

Storming the hilltop.
Then, from the barred yard, the children

Smell the melt of shoe-blacking,
Their faces turning, wordless and slow,

Their eyes opening
On a wonderful thing——

Six round black hats in the grass and a lozenge of wood,
And a naked mouth, red and awkward.

For a minute the sky pours into the hole like plasma.
There is no hope, it is given up.

Ariel

Stasis in darkness.
Then the substanceless blue
Pour of tor and distances.

God's lioness,
How one we grow,
Pivot of heels and knees!—The furrow

Splits and passes, sister to
The brown arc
Of the neck I cannot catch,

Nigger-eye
Berries cast dark
Hooks——

Black sweet blood mouthfuls,
Shadows.
Something else

Hauls me through air——
Thighs, hair;
Flakes from my heels.

White
Godiva, I unpeel——
Dead hands, dead stringencies.

And now I
Foam to wheat, a glitter of seas.
The child's cry

Melts in the wall.
And I
Am the arrow,

The dew that flies
Suicidal, at one with the drive
Into the red

Eye, the cauldron of morning.

Death & Co.

Two, of course there are two.
It seems perfectly natural now——
The one who never looks up, whose eyes are lidded
And balled, like Blake's,
Who exhibits

The birthmarks that are his trademark——
The scald scar of water,
The nude
Verdigris of the condor.
I am red meat. His beak

Claps sidewise: I am not his yet.
He tells me how badly I photograph.
He tells me how sweet
The babies look in their hospital
Icebox, a simple

Frill at the neck,
Then the flutings of their Ionian
Death-gowns,
Then two little feet.
He does not smile or smoke.

The other does that,
His hair long and plausive.
Bastard
Masturbating a glitter,
He wants to be loved.

I do not stir.
The frost makes a flower,
The dew makes a star,
The dead bell,
The dead bell.

Somebody's done for.

Lesbos

Viciousness in the kitchen!
The potatoes hiss.
It is all Hollywood, windowless,
The fluorescent light wincing on and off like a terrible
    migraine,
Coy paper strips for doors——
Stage curtains, a widow's frizz.
And I, love, am a pathological liar,
And my child—look at her, face down on the floor,
Little unstrung puppet, kicking to disappear——
Why she is schizophrenic,
Her face red and white, a panic,
You have stuck her kittens outside your window
In a sort of cement well
Where they crap and puke and cry and she can't hear.
You say you can't stand her,
The bastard's a girl.
You who have blown your tubes like a bad radio
Clear of voices and history, the staticky
Noise of the new.
You say I should drown the kittens. Their smell!
You say I should drown my girl.
She'll cut her throat at ten if she's mad at two.
The baby smiles, fat snail,
From the polished lozenges of orange linoleum.
You could eat him. He's a boy.
You say your husband is just no good to you.
His Jew-Mama guards his sweet sex like a pearl.

You have one baby, I have two.
I should sit on a rock off Cornwall and comb my hair.
I should wear tiger pants, I should have an affair.
We should meet in another life, we should meet in air,
Me and you.

Meanwhile there's a stink of fat and baby crap.
I'm doped and thick from my last sleeping pill.
The smog of cooking, the smog of hell
Floats our heads, two venomous opposites,
Our bones, our hair.
I call you Orphan, orphan. You are ill.
The sun gives you ulcers, the wind gives you T.B.
Once you were beautiful.
In New York, in Hollywood, the men said: "Through?
Gee baby, you are rare."
You acted, acted, acted for the thrill.
The impotent husband slumps out for a coffee.
I try to keep him in,
An old pole for the lightning,
The acid baths, the skyfuls off of you.
He lumps it down the plastic cobbled hill,
Flogged trolley. The sparks are blue.
The blue sparks spill,
Splitting like quartz into a million bits.

O jewel! O valuable!
That night the moon
Dragged its blood bag, sick
Animal
Up over the harbor lights.

And then grew normal,
Hard and apart and white.
The scale-sheen on the sand scared me to death.
We kept picking up handfuls, loving it,
Working it like dough, a mulatto body,
The silk grits.
A dog picked up your doggy husband. He went on.

Now I am silent, hate
Up to my neck,
Thick, thick.
I do not speak.
I am packing the hard potatoes like good clothes,
I am packing the babies,
I am packing the sick cats.
O vase of acid,
It is love you are full of. You know who you hate.
He is hugging his ball and chain down by the gate
That opens to the sea
Where it drives in, white and black,
Then spews it back.
Every day you fill him with soul-stuff, like a pitcher.
You are so exhausted.
Your voice my ear-ring,
Flapping and sucking, blood-loving bat.
That is that. That is that.
You peer from the door,
Sad hag. "Every woman's a whore.
I can't communicate."

I see your cute décor
Close on you like the fist of a baby

Or an anemone, that sea
Sweetheart, that kleptomaniac.
I am still raw.
I say I may be back.
You know what lies are for.

Even in your Zen heaven we shan't meet.

Nick and the Candlestick

I am a miner. The light burns blue.
Waxy stalactites
Drip and thicken, tears

The earthen womb
Exudes from its dead boredom.
Black bat airs

Wrap me, raggy shawls,
Cold homicides.
They weld to me like plums.

Old cave of calcium
Icicles, old echoer.
Even the newts are white,

Those holy Joes.
And the fish, the fish——
Christ! They are panes of ice,

A vice of knives,
A piranha
Religion, drinking

It's first communion out of my live toes.
The candle
Gulps and recovers its small altitude,

Its yellows hearten.
O love, how did you get here?
O embryo

Remembering, even in sleep,
Your crossed position.
The blood blooms clean

In you, ruby.
The pain
You wake to is not yours.

Love, love,
I have hung our cave with roses.
With soft rugs——

The last of Victoriana.
Let the stars
Plummet to their dark address,

Let the mercuric
Atoms that cripple drip
Into the terrible well,

You are the one
Solid the spaces lean on, envious.
You are the baby in the barn.

Gulliver

Over your body the clouds go
High, high and icily
And a little flat, as if they

Floated on a glass that was invisible.
Unlike swans,
Having no reflections;

Unlike you,
With no strings attached.
All cool, all blue. Unlike you——

You, there on your back,
Eyes to the sky.
The spider-men have caught you,

Winding and twining their petty fetters,
Their bribes——
So many silks.

How they hate you.
They converse in the valley of your fingers, they are
    inchworms.
They would have you sleep in their cabinets,

This toe and that toe, a relic.
Step off!
Step off seven leagues, like those distances

That revolve in Crivelli, untouchable.
Let this eye be an eagle,
The shadow of this lip, an abyss.

Getting There

How far is it?
How far is it now?
The gigantic gorilla interiors
Of the wheels move, they appal me——
The terrible brains
Of Krupp, black muzzles
Revolving, the sound
Punching out Absence! like cannon.
It is Russia I have to get across, it is some war or other.
I am dragging my body
Quietly through the straw of the boxcars.
Now is the time for bribery.
What do wheels eat, these wheels
Fixed to their arcs like gods,
The silver leash of the will——
Inexorable. And their pride!
All the gods know is destinations.
I am a letter in this slot——
I fly to a name, two eyes.
Will there be fire, will there be bread?
Here there is such mud.
It is a trainstop, the nurses
Undergoing the faucet water, its veils, veils in a nunnery,
Touching their wounded,
The men the blood still pumps forward,
Legs, arms piled outside
The tent of unending cries——
A hospital of dolls.

And the men, what is left of the men
Pumped ahead by these pistons, this blood
Into the next mile,
The next hour——
Dynasty of broken arrows!
How far is it?
There is mud on my feet,
Thick, red and slipping. It is Adam's side,
This earth I rise from, and I in agony.
I cannot undo myself, and the train is steaming.
Steaming and breathing, its teeth
Ready to roll, like a devil's.
There is a minute at the end of it
A minute, a dewdrop.
How far is it?
It is so small
The place I am getting to, why are there these obstacles——
The body of this woman,
Charred skirts and deathmask
Mourned by religious figures, by garlanded children.
And now detonations——
Thunder and guns.
The fire's between us.
Is there no still place
Turning and turning in the middle air,
Untouched and untouchable.
The train is dragging itself, it is screaming——
An animal
Insane for the destination,
The bloodspot,
The face at the end of the flare.
I shall bury the wounded like pupas,

I shall count and bury the dead.
Let their souls writhe in a dew,
Incense in my track.
The carriages rock, they are cradles.
And I, stepping from this skin
Of old bandages, boredoms, old faces

Step to you from the black car of Lethe,
Pure as a baby.

Medusa

Off that landspit of stony mouth-plugs,
Eyes rolled by white sticks,
Ears cupping the sea's incoherences,
You house your unnerving head—God-ball,
Lens of mercies,

Your stooges
Plying their wild cells in my keel's shadow,
Pushing by like hearts,
Red stigmata at the very centre,
Riding the rip tide to the nearest point of departure,

Dragging their Jesus hair.
Did I escape, I wonder?
My mind winds to you
Old barnacled umbilicus, Atlantic cable,
Keeping itself, it seems, in a state of miraculous repair.

In any case, you are always there,
Tremulous breath at the end of my line,
Curve of water upleaping
To my water rod, dazzling and grateful,
Touching and sucking.

I didn't call you.
I didn't call you at all.

Nevertheless, nevertheless
You steamed to me over the sea,
Fat and red, a placenta
Paralyzing the kicking lovers.
Cobra light
Squeezing the breath from the blood bells
Of the fuchsia. I could draw no breath,
Dead and moneyless,

Overexposed, like an X-ray.
Who do you think you are?
A Communion wafer? Blubbery Mary?
I shall take no bite of your body,
Bottle in which I live,

Ghastly Vatican.
I am sick to death of hot salt.
Green as eunuchs, your wishes
Hiss at my sins.
Off, off, eely tentacle!

There is nothing between us.

The Moon and the Yew Tree

This is the light of the mind, cold and planetary.
The trees of the mind are black. The light is blue.
The grasses unload their griefs on my feet as if I were God,
Prickling my ankles and murmuring of their humility.
Fumy, spiritous mists inhabit this place
Separated from my house by a row of headstones.
I simply cannot see where there is to get to.

The moon is no door. It is a face in its own right,
White as a knuckle and terribly upset.
It drags the sea after it like a dark crime; it is quiet
With the O-gape of complete despair. I live here.
Twice on Sunday, the bells startle the sky——
Eight great tongues affirming the Resurrection.
At the end, they soberly bong out their names.

The yew tree points up. It has a Gothic shape.
The eyes lift after it and find the moon.
The moon is my mother. She is not sweet like Mary.
Her blue garments unloose small bats and owls.
How I would like to believe in tenderness——
The face of the effigy, gentled by candles,
Bending, on me in particular, its mild eyes.

I have fallen a long way. Clouds are flowering
Blue and mystical over the face of the stars.
Inside the church, the saints will be all blue,

Floating on their delicate feet over the cold pews,
Their hands and faces stiff with holiness.
The moon sees nothing of this. She is bald and wild.
And the message of the yew tree is blackness—blackness and
    silence.

A Birthday Present

What is this, behind this veil, is it ugly, is it beautiful?
It is shimmering, has it breasts, has it edges?

I am sure it is unique, I am sure it is just what I want.
When I am quiet at my cooking I feel it looking, I feel it
    thinking

"Is this the one I am to appear for,
Is this the elect one, the one with black eye-pits and a scar?

Measuring the flour, cutting off the surplus,
Adhering to rules, to rules, to rules.

Is this the one for the annunciation?
My god, what a laugh!"

But it shimmers, it does not stop, and I think it wants me.
I would not mind if it was bones, or a pearl button.

I do not want much of a present, anyway, this year.
After all I am alive only by accident.

I would have killed myself gladly that time any possible way.
Now there are these veils, shimmering like curtains,

The diaphanous satins of a January window
White as babies' bedding and glittering with dead breath.
  O ivory!

It must be a tusk there, a ghost-column.
Can you not see I do not mind what it is?

Can you not give it to me?
Do not be ashamed—I do not mind if it is small.

Do not be mean, I am ready for enormity.
Let us sit down to it, one on either side, admiring the gleam,

The glaze, the mirrory variety of it.
Let us eat our supper at it, like a hospital plate.

I know why you will not give it to me,
You are terrified

The world will go up in a shriek, and your head with it,
Bossed, brazen, an antique shield,

A marvel to your great-grandchildren.
Do not be afraid, it is not so.

I will only take it and go aside quietly.
You will not even hear me opening it, no paper crackle,

No falling ribbons, no scream at the end.
I do not think you credit me with this discretion.

If you only knew how the veils were killing my days.
To you they are only transparencies, clear air.

But my god, the clouds are like cotton.
Armies of them. They are carbon monoxide.

Sweetly, sweetly I breathe in,
Filling my veins with invisibles, with the million

Probable motes that tick the years off my life.
You are silver-suited for the occasion. O adding machine——

Is it impossible for you to let something go and have it go
    whole?
Must you stamp each piece in purple,

Must you kill what you can?
There is this one thing I want today, and only you can
    give it to me.

It stands at my window, big as the sky.
It breathes from my sheets, the cold dead centre

Where spilt lives congeal and stiffen to history.
Let it not come by the mail, finger by finger.

Let it not come by word of mouth, I should be sixty
By the time the whole of it was delivered, and too numb
    to use it.

Only let down the veil, the veil, the veil.
If it were death

I would admire the deep gravity of it, its timeless eyes.
I would know you were serious.

There would be a nobility then, there would be a birthday.
And the knife not carve, but enter

Pure and clean as the cry of a baby,
And the universe slide from my side.

Mary's Song

The Sunday lamb cracks in its fat.
The fat
Sacrifices its opacity. . . .

A window, holy gold.
The fire makes it precious,
The same fire

Melting the tallow heretics,
Ousting the Jews.
Their thick palls float

Over the cicatrix of Poland, burnt-out
Germany.
They do not die.

Grey birds obsess my heart,
Mouth-ash, ash of eye.
They settle. On the high

Precipice
That emptied one man into space
The ovens glowed like heavens, incandescent.

It is a heart,
This holocaust I walk in,
O golden child the world will kill and eat.

Letter in November

Love, the world
Suddenly turns, turns colour. The streetlight
Splits through the rat's-tail
Pods of the laburnum at nine in the morning.
It is the Arctic,

This little black
Circle, with its tawn silk grasses—babies' hair.
There is a green in the air,
Soft, delectable.
It cushions me lovingly.

I am flushed and warm.
I think I may be enormous,
I am so stupidly happy,
My Wellingtons
Squelching and squelching through the beautiful red.

This is my property.
Two times a day
I pace it, sniffing
The barbarous holly with its viridian
Scallops, pure iron,

And the wall of old corpses.
I love them.
I love them like history.
The apples are golden,
Imagine it——

My seventy trees
Holding their gold-ruddy balls
In a thick grey death-soup,
Their million
Gold leaves metal and breathless.

O love, O celibate.
Nobody but me
Walks the waist-high wet.
The irreplaceable
Golds bleed and deepen, the mouths of Thermopylae.

The Rival

If the moon smiled, she would resemble you.
You leave the same impression
Of something beautiful, but annihilating.
Both of you are great light borrowers.
Her O-mouth grieves at the world; yours is unaffected,

And your first gift is making stone out of everything.
I wake to a mausoleum; you are here,
Ticking your fingers on the marble table, looking for
    cigarettes,
Spiteful as a woman, but not so nervous,
And dying to say something unanswerable.

The moon, too, abases her subjects,
But in the daytime she is ridiculous.
Your dissatisfactions, on the other hand,
Arrive through the mailslot with loving regularity,
White and blank, expansive as carbon monoxide.

No day is safe from news of you,
Walking about in Africa maybe, but thinking of me.

Daddy

You do not do, you do not do
Any more, black shoe
In which I have lived like a foot
For thirty years, poor and white,
Barely daring to breathe or Achoo.

Daddy, I have had to kill you.
You died before I had time——
Marble-heavy, a bag full of God,
Ghastly statue with one grey toe
Big as a Frisco seal

And a head in the freakish Atlantic
Where it pours bean green over blue
In the waters off beautiful Nauset.
I used to pray to recover you.
Ach, du.

In the German tongue, in the Polish town
Scraped flat by the roller
Of wars, wars, wars.
But the name of the town is common.
My Polack friend

Says there are a dozen or two.
So I never could tell where you
Put your foot, your root,
I never could talk to you.
The tongue stuck in my jaw.

It stuck in a barb wire snare.
Ich, ich, ich, ich,
I could hardly speak.
I thought every German was you.
And the language obscene

An engine, an engine
Chuffing me off like a Jew.
A Jew to Dachau, Auschwitz, Belsen.
I began to talk like a Jew.
I think I may well be a Jew.

The snows of the Tyrol, the clear beer of Vienna
Are not very pure or true.
With my gypsy ancestress and my weird luck
And my Taroc pack and my Taroc pack
I may be a bit of a Jew.

I have always been scared of *you*,
With your Luftwaffe, your gobbledygoo.
And your neat moustache
And your Aryan eye, bright blue.
Panzer-man, panzer-man, O You——

Not God but a swastika
So black no sky could squeak through.
Every woman adores a Fascist,
The boot in the face, the brute
Brute heart of a brute like you.

You stand at the blackboard, daddy,
In the picture I have of you,
A cleft in your chin instead of your foot
But no less a devil for that, no not
Any less the black man who

Bit my pretty red heart in two.
I was ten when they buried you.
At twenty I tried to die
And get back, back, back to you.
I thought even the bones would do.

But they pulled me out of the sack,
And they stuck me together with glue.
And then I knew what to do.
I made a model of you,
A man in black with a Meinkampf look

And a love of the rack and the screw.
And I said I do, I do.
So daddy, I'm finally through.
The black telephone's off at the root,
The voices just can't worm through.

If I've killed one man, I've killed two——
The vampire who said he was you
And drank my blood for a year,
Seven years, if you want to know.
Daddy, you can lie back now.

There's a stake in your fat black heart
And the villagers never liked you.
They are dancing and stamping on you.
They always *knew* it was you.
Daddy, daddy, you bastard, I'm through.

You're

❦

Clownlike, happiest on your hands,
Feet to the stars, and moon-skulled,
Gilled like a fish. A common-sense
Thumbs-down on the dodo's mode.
Wrapped up in yourself like a spool,
Trawling your dark as owls do.
Mute as a turnip from the Fourth
Of July to All Fools' Day,
O high-riser, my little loaf.

Vague as fog and looked for like mail.
Farther off than Australia.
Bent-backed Atlas, our travelled prawn.
Snug as a bud and at home
Like a sprat in a pickle jug.
A creel of eels, all ripples.
Jumpy as a Mexican bean.
Right, like a well-done sum.
A clean slate, with your own face on.

Fever 103°

Pure? What does it mean?
The tongues of hell
Are dull, dull as the triple

Tongues of dull, fat Cerberus
Who wheezes at the gate. Incapable
Of licking clean

The aguey tendon, the sin, the sin.
The tinder cries.
The indelible smell

Of a snuffed candle!
Love, love, the low smokes roll
From me like Isadora's scarves, I'm in a fright

One scarf will catch and anchor in the wheel.
Such yellow sullen smokes
Make their own element. They will not rise,

But trundle round the globe
Choking the aged and the meek,
The weak

Hothouse baby in its crib,
The ghastly orchid
Hanging its hanging garden in the air,

Devilish leopard!
Radiation turned it white
And killed it in an hour.

Greasing the bodies of adulterers
Like Hiroshima ash and eating in.
The sin. The sin.

Darling, all night
I have been flickering, off, on, off, on.
The sheets grow heavy as a lecher's kiss.

Three days. Three nights.
Lemon water, chicken
Water, water make me retch.

I am too pure for you or anyone.
Your body
Hurts me as the world hurts God. I am a lantern——

My head a moon
Of Japanese paper, my gold beaten skin
Infinitely delicate and infinitely expensive.

Does not my heat astound you. And my light.
All by myself I am a huge camellia
Glowing and coming and going, flush on flush.

I think I am going up,
I think I may rise——
The beads of hot metal fly, and I, love, I

Am a pure acetylene
Virgin
Attended by roses,

By kisses, by cherubim,
By whatever these pink things mean.
Not you, nor him

Not him, nor him
(My selves dissolving, old whore petticoats)——
To Paradise.

The Bee Meeting

❧

Who are these people at the bridge to meet me? They are the
 villagers——
The rector, the midwife, the sexton, the agent for bees.
In my sleeveless summery dress I have no protection,
And they are all gloved and covered, why did nobody tell me?
They are smiling and taking out veils tacked to ancient hats.

I am nude as a chicken neck, does nobody love me?
Yes, here is the secretary of bees with her white shop smock,
Buttoning the cuffs at my wrists and the slit from my neck to
 my knees.
Now I am milkweed silk, the bees will not notice.
They will not smell my fear, my fear, my fear.

Which is the rector now, is it that man in black?
Which is the midwife, is that her blue coat?
Everybody is nodding a square black head, they are knights in
 visors,
Breastplates of cheesecloth knotted under the armpits.
Their smiles and their voices are changing. I am led through a
 beanfield.

Strips of tinfoil winking like people,
Feather dusters fanning their hands in a sea of bean flowers,
Creamy bean flowers with black eyes and leaves like bored
 hearts.

Is it blood clots the tendrils are dragging up that string?
No, no, it is scarlet flowers that will one day be edible.

Now they are giving me a fashionable white straw Italian hat
And a black veil that moulds to my face, they are making me
    one of them.
They are leading me to the shorn grove, the circle of hives.
Is it the hawthorn that smells so sick?
The barren body of hawthorn, etherizing its children.

Is it some operation that is taking place?
It is the surgeon my neighbours are waiting for,
This apparition in a green helmet,
Shining gloves and white suit.
Is it the butcher, the grocer, the postman, someone I know?

I cannot run, I am rooted, and the gorse hurts me
With its yellow purses, its spiky armoury.
I could not run without having to run forever.
The white hive is snug as a virgin,
Sealing off her brood cells, her honey, and quietly humming.

Smoke rolls and scarves in the grove.
The mind of the hive thinks this is the end of everything.
Here they come, the outriders, on their hysterical elastics.
If I stand very still, they will think I am cow parsley,
A gullible head untouched by their animosity,

Not even nodding, a personage in a hedgerow.
The villagers open the chambers, they are hunting the queen.

Is she hiding, is she eating honey? She is very clever.
She is old, old, old, she must live another year, and she
  knows it.
While in their fingerjoint cells the new virgins

Dream of a duel they will win inevitably,
A curtain of wax dividing them from the bride flight,
The upflight of the murderess into a heaven that loves her.
The villagers are moving the virgins, there will be no killing.
The old queen does not show herself, is she so ungrateful?

I am exhausted, I am exhausted——
Pillar of white in a blackout of knives.
I am the magician's girl who does not flinch.
The villagers are untying their disguises, they are shaking
  hands.
Whose is that long white box in the grove, what have they
  accomplished, why am I cold?

The Arrival of the Bee Box

I ordered this, this clean wood box
Square as a chair and almost too heavy to lift.
I would say it was the coffin of a midget
Or a square baby
Were there not such a din in it.

The box is locked, it is dangerous.
I have to live with it overnight
And I can't keep away from it.
There are no windows, so I can't see what is in there.
There is only a little grid, no exit.

I put my eye to the grid.
It is dark, dark,
With the swarmy feeling of African hands
Minute and shrunk for export,
Black on black, angrily clambering.

How can I let them out?
It is the noise that appals me most of all,
The unintelligible syllables.
It is like a Roman mob,
Small, taken one by one, but my god, together!

I lay my ear to furious Latin.
I am not a Caesar.
I have simply ordered a box of maniacs.
They can be sent back.
They can die, I need feed them nothing, I am the owner.

I wonder how hungry they are.
I wonder if they would forget me
If I just undid the locks and stood back and turned into a tree.
There is the laburnum, its blond colonnades,
And the petticoats of the cherry.

They might ignore me immediately
In my moon suit and funeral veil.
I am no source of honey
So why should they turn on me?
Tomorrow I will be sweet God, I will set them free.

The box is only temporary.

Stings

Bare-handed, I hand the combs.
The man in white smiles, bare-handed,
Our cheesecloth gauntlets neat and sweet,
The throats of our wrists brave lilies.
He and I

Have a thousand clean cells between us,
Eight combs of yellow cups,
And the hive itself a teacup,
White with pink flowers on it,
With excessive love I enamelled it

Thinking "Sweetness, sweetness."
Brood cells grey as the fossils of shells
Terrify me, they seem so old.
What am I buying, wormy mahogany?
Is there any queen at all in it?

If there is, she is old,
Her wings torn shawls, her long body
Rubbed of its plush——
Poor and bare and unqueenly and even shameful.
I stand in a column

Of winged, unmiraculous women,
Honey-drudgers.
I am no drudge
Though for years I have eaten dust
And dried plates with my dense hair.

And seen my strangeness evaporate,
Blue dew from dangerous skin.
Will they hate me,
These women who only scurry,
Whose news is the open cherry, the open clover?

It is almost over.
I am in control.
Here is my honey-machine,
It will work without thinking,
Opening, in spring, like an industrious virgin

To scour the creaming crests
As the moon, for its ivory powders, scours the sea.
A third person is watching.
He has nothing to do with the bee-seller or with me.
Now he is gone

In eight great bounds, a great scapegoat.
Here is his slipper, here is another,
And here the square of white linen
He wore instead of a hat.
He was sweet,

The sweat of his efforts a rain
Tugging the world to fruit.
The bees found him out,
Moulding onto his lips like lies,
Complicating his features.

They thought death was worth it, but I
Have a self to recover, a queen.
Is she dead, is she sleeping?
Where has she been,
With her lion-red body, her wings of glass?

Now she is flying
More terrible than she ever was, red
Scar in the sky, red comet
Over the engine that killed her——
The mausoleum, the wax house.

The Swarm

Somebody is shooting at something in our town——
A dull pom, pom in the Sunday street.
Jealousy can open the blood,
It can make black roses.
Who are they shooting at?

It is you the knives are out for
At Waterloo, Waterloo, Napoleon,
The hump of Elba on your short back,
And the snow, marshalling its brilliant cutlery
Mass after mass, saying Shh!

Shh! These are chess people you play with,
Still figures of ivory.
The mud squirms with throats,
Stepping stones for French bootsoles.
The gilt and pink domes of Russia melt and float off

In the furnace of greed. Clouds, clouds.
So the swarm balls and deserts
Seventy feet up, in a black pine tree.
It must be shot down. Pom! Pom!
So dumb it thinks bullets are thunder.

It thinks they are the voice of God
Condoning the beak, the claw, the grin of the dog
Yellow-haunched, a pack-dog,
Grinning over its bone of ivory
Like the pack, the pack, like everybody.

The bees have got so far. Seventy feet high!
Russia, Poland and Germany!
The mild hills, the same old magenta
Fields shrunk to a penny
Spun into a river, the river crossed.

The bees argue, in their black ball,
A flying hedgehog, all prickles.
The man with grey hands stands under the honeycomb
Of their dream, the hived station
Where trains, faithful to their steel arcs,

Leave and arrive, and there is no end to the country.
Pom! Pom! They fall
Dismembered, to a tod of ivy.
So much for the charioteers, the outriders, the Grand Army!
A red tatter, Napoleon!

The last badge of victory.
The swarm is knocked into a cocked straw hat.
Elba, Elba, bleb on the sea!
The white busts of marshals, admirals, generals
Worming themselves into niches.

How instructive this is!
The dumb, banded bodies
Walking the plank draped with Mother France's upholstery
Into a new mausoleum,
An ivory palace, a crotch pine.

The man with grey hands smiles——
The smile of a man of business, intensely practical.
They are not hands at all
But asbestos receptacles.
Pom! Pom! "They would have killed *me*."

Stings big as drawing pins!
It seems bees have a notion of honour,
A black, intractable mind.
Napoleon is pleased, he is pleased with everything.
O Europe! O ton of honey!

Wintering

This is the easy time, there is nothing doing.
I have whirled the midwife's extractor,
I have my honey,
Six jars of it,
Six cat's eyes in the wine cellar,

Wintering in a dark without window
At the heart of the house
Next to the last tenant's rancid jam
And the bottles of empty glitters——
Sir So-and-so's gin.

This is the room I have never been in.
This is the room I could never breathe in.
The black bunched in there like a bat,
No light
But the torch and its faint

Chinese yellow on appalling objects——
Black asininity. Decay.
Possession.
It is they who own me.
Neither cruel nor indifferent,

Only ignorant.
This is the time of hanging on for the bees—the bees
So slow I hardly know them,
Filing like soldiers
To the syrup tin

To make up for the honey I've taken.
Tate and Lyle keeps them going,
The refined snow.
It is Tate and Lyle they live on, instead of flowers.
They take it. The cold sets in.

Now they ball in a mass,
Black
Mind against all that white.
The smile of the snow is white.
It spreads itself out, a mile-long body of Meissen,

Into which, on warm days,
They can only carry their dead.
The bees are all women,
Maids and the long royal lady.
They have got rid of the men,

The blunt, clumsy stumblers, the boors.
Winter is for women——
The woman, still at her knitting,
At the cradle of Spanish walnut,
Her body a bulb in the cold and too dumb to think.

Will the hive survive, will the gladiolas
Succeed in banking their fires
To enter another year?
What will they taste of, the Christmas roses?
The bees are flying. They taste the spring.

The Hanging Man

By the roots of my hair some god got hold of me.
I sizzled in his blue volts like a desert prophet.

The nights snapped out of sight like a lizard's eyelid:
A world of bald white days in a shadeless socket.

A vulturous boredom pinned me in this tree.
If he were I, he would do what I did.

Little Fugue

The yew's black fingers wag;
Cold clouds go over.
So the deaf and dumb
Signal the blind, and are ignored.

I like black statements.
The featurelessness of that cloud, now!
White as an eye all over!
The eye of the blind pianist

At my table on the ship.
He felt for his food.
His fingers had the noses of weasels.
I couldn't stop looking.

He could hear Beethoven:
Black yew, white cloud,
The horrific complications.
Finger-traps—a tumult of keys.

Empty and silly as plates,
So the blind smile.
I envy the big noises,
The yew hedge of the Grosse Fuge.

Deafness is something else.
Such a dark funnel, my father!

I see your voice
Black and leafy, as in my childhood,

A yew hedge of orders,
Gothic and barbarous, pure German.
Dead men cry from it.
I am guilty of nothing.

The yew my Christ, then.
Is it not as tortured?
And you, during the Great War
In the California delicatessen

Lopping the sausages!
They colour my sleep,
Red, mottled, like cut necks.
There was a silence!

Great silence of another order.
I was seven, I knew nothing.
The world occurred.
You had one leg, and a Prussian mind.

Now similar clouds
Are spreading their vacuous sheets.
Do you say nothing?
I am lame in the memory.

I remember a blue eye,
A briefcase of tangerines.
This was a man, then!
Death opened, like a black tree, blackly.

I survive the while,
Arranging my morning.
These are my fingers, this my baby.
The clouds are a marriage dress, of that pallor.

Years

They enter as animals from the outer
Space of holly where spikes
Are not the thoughts I turn on, like a Yogi,
But greenness, darkness so pure
They freeze and are.

O God, I am not like you
In your vacuous black,
Stars stuck all over, bright stupid confetti.
Eternity bores me,
I never wanted it.

What I love is
The piston in motion——
My soul dies before it.
And the hooves of the horses,
Their merciless churn.

And you, great Stasis——
What is so great in that!
Is it a tiger this year, this roar at the door?
Is it a Christus,
The awful

God-bit in him
Dying to fly and be done with it?
The blood berries are themselves, they are very still.

The hooves will not have it,
In blue distance the pistons hiss.

The Munich Mannequins

Perfection is terrible, it cannot have children.
Cold as snow breath, it tamps the womb

Where the yew trees blow like hydras,
The tree of life and the tree of life

Unloosing their moons, month after month, to no purpose.
The blood flood is the flood of love,

The absolute sacrifice.
It means: no more idols but me,

Me and you.
So, in their sulphur loveliness, in their smiles

These mannequins lean tonight
In Munich, morgue between Paris and Rome,

Naked and bald in their furs,
Orange lollies on silver sticks,

Intolerable, without mind.
The snow drops its pieces of darkness,

Nobody's about. In the hotels
Hands will be opening doors and setting

Down shoes for a polish of carbon
Into which broad toes will go tomorrow.

O the domesticity of these windows,
The baby lace, the green-leaved confectionery,

The thick Germans slumbering in their bottomless Stolz.
And the black phones on hooks

Glittering
Glittering and digesting

Voicelessness. The snow has no voice.

Totem

The engine is killing the track, the track is silver,
It stretches into the distance. It will be eaten nevertheless.

Its running is useless.
At nightfall there is the beauty of drowned fields,

Dawn gilds the farmers like pigs,
Swaying slightly in their thick suits,

White towers of Smithfield ahead,
Fat haunches and blood on their minds.

There is no mercy in the glitter of cleavers,
The butcher's guillotine that whispers: "How's this, how's
    this?"

In the bowl the hare is aborted,
Its baby head out of the way, embalmed in spice,

Flayed of fur and humanity.
Let us eat it like Plato's afterbirth,

Let us eat it like Christ.
These are the people that were important——

Their round eyes, their teeth, their grimaces
On a stick that rattles and clicks, a counterfeit snake.

Shall the hood of the cobra appal me——
The loneliness of its eye, the eye of the mountains

Through which the sky eternally threads itself?
The world is blood-hot and personal

Dawn says, with its blood-flush.
There is no terminus, only suitcases

Out of which the same self unfolds like a suit
Bald and shiny, with pockets of wishes,

Notions and tickets, short circuits and folding mirrors.
I am mad, calls the spider, waving its many arms.

And in truth it is terrible,
Multiplied in the eyes of the flies.

They buzz like blue children
In nets of the infinite,

Roped in at the end by the one
Death with its many sticks.

Paralytic

It happens. Will it go on?——
My mind a rock,
No fingers to grip, no tongue,
My god the iron lung

That loves me, pumps
My two
Dust bags in and out,
Will not

Let me relapse
While the day outside glides by like ticker tape.
The night brings violets,
Tapestries of eyes,

Lights,
The soft anonymous
Talkers: "You all right?"
The starched, inaccessible breast.

Dead egg, I lie
Whole
On a whole world I cannot touch,
At the white, tight

Drum of my sleeping couch
Photographs visit me——
My wife, dead and flat, in 1920 furs,
Mouth full of pearls,

Two girls
As flat as she, who whisper "We're your daughters."
The still waters
Wrap my lips,

Eyes, nose and ears,
A clear
Cellophane I cannot crack.
On my bare back

I smile, a buddha, all
Wants, desire
Falling from me like rings
Hugging their lights.

The claw
Of the magnolia,
Drunk on its own scents,
Asks nothing of life.

Balloons

Since Christmas they have lived with us,
Guileless and clear,
Oval soul-animals,
Taking up half the space,
Moving and rubbing on the silk

Invisible air drifts,
Giving a shriek and pop
When attacked, then scooting to rest, barely trembling.
Yellow cathead, blue fish——
Such queer moons we live with

Instead of dead furniture!
Straw mats, white walls
And these travelling
Globes of thin air, red, green,
Delighting

The heart like wishes or free
Peacocks blessing
Old ground with a feather
Beaten in starry metals.
Your small

Brother is making
His balloon squeak like a cat.
Seeming to see
A funny pink world he might eat on the other side of it,
He bites,

Then sits
Back, fat jug
Contemplating a world clear as water,
A red
Shred in his little fist.

Poppies in July

Little poppies, little hell flames,
Do you do no harm?

You flicker. I cannot touch you.
I put my hands among the flames. Nothing burns.

And it exhausts me to watch you
Flickering like that, wrinkly and clear red, like the skin
  of a mouth.

A mouth just bloodied.
Little bloody skirts!

There are fumes that I cannot touch.
Where are your opiates, your nauseous capsules?

If I could bleed, or sleep!——
If my mouth could marry a hurt like that!

Or your liquors seep to me, in this glass capsule,
Dulling and stilling.

But colourless. Colourless.

Kindness

Kindness glides about my house.
Dame Kindness, she is so nice!
The blue and red jewels of her rings smoke
In the windows, the mirrors
Are filling with smiles.

What is so real as the cry of a child?
A rabbit's cry may be wilder
But it has no soul.
Sugar can cure everything, so Kindness says.
Sugar is a necessary fluid,

Its crystals a little poultice.
O kindness, kindness
Sweetly picking up pieces!
My Japanese silks, desperate butterflies,
May be pinned any minute, anaesthetized.

And here you come, with a cup of tea
Wreathed in steam.
The blood jet is poetry,
There is no stopping it.
You hand me two children, two roses.

Contusion

Colour floods to the spot, dull purple.
The rest of the body is all washed out,
The colour of pearl.

In a pit of rock
The sea sucks obsessively,
One hollow the whole sea's pivot.

The size of a fly,
The doom mark
Crawls down the wall.

The heart shuts,
The sea slides back,
The mirrors are sheeted.

Edge

❧

The woman is perfected.
Her dead

Body wears the smile of accomplishment,
The illusion of a Greek necessity

Flows in the scrolls of her toga,
Her bare

Feet seem to be saying:
We have come so far, it is over.

Each dead child coiled, a white serpent,
One at each little

Pitcher of milk, now empty.
She has folded

Them back into her body as petals
Of a rose close when the garden

Stiffens and odours bleed
From the sweet, deep throats of the night flower.

The moon has nothing to be sad about,
Staring from her hood of bone.

She is used to this sort of thing.
Her blacks crackle and drag.

Words

Axes
After whose stroke the wood rings,
And the echoes!
Echoes travelling
Off from the centre like horses.

The sap
Wells like tears, like the
Water striving
To re-establish its mirror
Over the rock

That drops and turns,
A white skull,
Eaten by weedy greens.
Years later I
Encounter them on the road——

Words dry and riderless,
The indefatigable hoof-taps.
While
From the bottom of the pool, fixed stars
Govern a life.

About Sylvia Plath

More than three decades after her death, Sylvia Plath's writings continue to inspire and provoke. Her only novel, *The Bell Jar,* remains a classic of American fiction, and her volumes of poetry—*The Colossus* (1960), *Ariel* (1965), *Crossing the Water* (1971), *Winter Trees* (1971), and *The Collected Poems* (1981)—have placed her among this century's essential American poets.

Sylvia Plath was born on October 27, 1932, in Jamaica Plain, Massachusetts. Her father, Otto Plath, was a professor of biology at Boston University and an internationally recognized expert on bees. Her mother, Aurelia Schober Plath, was a teacher. When Sylvia was four years old, the family moved to Winthrop, Massachusetts, a peninsular seaside town to the northeast of Boston. Plath would later recall her four years in Winthrop as a time defined by the sea; every aspect of her childhood there seemed connected in some way with salt spray and ocean air. "When I was learning to creep," she recalled years later, "my mother set me down on the beach to see what I thought of it. I crawled straight for the coming wave and was just through the wall of green when she caught my heels."

On November 5, 1940, when Plath was eight years old, her father died. Otto Plath and his death would haunt his daughter's remaining years—and her poetry. The figure of the father as beekeeper, tyrant, deserter, or vicious "panzer-man" "with a Meinkampf look" appears throughout Plath's poetry, culminating in the poem "Daddy," written only a few months before her death.

The most immediate practical consequence of Otto Plath's death was the necessity faced by Aurelia Plath of finding a way to support herself and her two children. Together with her parents, Aurelia moved to the college town of Wellesley, Massachusetts. Mrs. Plath resumed her teaching career, in Boston University's medical-secretarial training program; her father found a position as maitre d'hotel at the Brookline Country Club (where he lived during the week); and her mother took over the care and running of the household. Plath's first published poem appeared about this time, in the *Boston Traveller*. And in school she was already establishing herself as a dedicated, fiercely competitive overachiever.

In high school Plath continued to drive herself—as a straight-A student, as a class leader, and as an aspiring poet. She submitted over forty-five stories and poems to the popular young women's magazine, *Seventeen,* through the early spring of 1950. Her persistence was rewarded not long after her graduation from high school: The August 1950 issue of *Seventeen* carried her first published story, "And Summer Will Not Come Again." And during that same summer, *The Christian Science Monitor* published her poem, "Bitter Strawberries."

Plath was nearly eighteen when she entered Smith College on two scholarships: one from the Wellesley-Smith Club, the other endowed by Olive Higgins Prouty, the author of *Stella Dallas* (and who later would become a friend and patron). In addition to excelling both academically and socially at Smith, Plath continued to write (reportedly more than four hundred poems in all during the Smith years), keeping herself to a firm regimen. And *Seventeen* continued to publish her stories and poems. In August 1951, her story, "Sunday at the Mintons," won *Mademoiselle* magazine's annual fiction contest. About this same time, Plath made her first reported attempt at suicide. Many years later, A. Alvarez, the British critic and poet, would argue that Plath's self-destructiveness was "the very source of her creative energy, . . . it was, precisely, a source of living energy, of her imaginative, creative power." Plath's readers and critics still struggle with that paradoxical union of self-destructiveness and creative energy that was at the core of her personality.

In the fall of 1952, during her junior year, Plath was awarded two Smith College prizes for poetry and was inducted into the college's honorary arts society and into Phi Beta Kappa. And early the following year *Harper's Magazine* bought three of her poems. From this time on, her poems appeared in prestigious magazines on both sides of the Atlantic—including *The New Yorker, Poetry,*

Mademoiselle, the *Hudson Review, The New Statesman, London Magazine, New American Review, Partisan Review,* the *Observer, Times Literary Supplement,* and *Transatlantic,* among others.

Plath's experiences during the summer of 1953 and the ensuing autumn and winter—as a guest editor at *Mademoiselle* in New York City and in deepening depression back home—provided the basis for her novel, *The Bell Jar.* Near that summer's end, she nearly succeeded in killing herself with a massive intake of sleeping pills. The harrowing sequence of events—from depression through electroshock and psychotherapy to re-established stability through which Esther Greenwood suffers in *The Bell Jar* is widely speculated to reflect the anguish experienced by Plath over those terrible several months. After treatment at McLean's Hospital in Massachusetts, she resumed her academic and literary endeavors. In preparation for returning to college, she spent the summer of 1954 taking courses at Harvard; and she returned to Smith that fall. After completing her honors thesis (on the double personality in Dostoyevsky's novels) and winning more poetry prizes, she graduated the following spring, *summa cum laude,* and set off for Newnham College, Cambridge, England, as a Fulbright Scholar.

It was at Cambridge, on February 26, 1956, that she first met poet Ted Hughes. "I met the strongest man in the world . . . with a voice like the thunder of God," she wrote in one journal entry. Plath and Hughes were married four months later, in June of 1956, in a private ceremony attended only by Plath's mother.

The next year Plath received her M.A. from Newn-
ham College—as well as *Poetry* magazine's Bess Hokin
Award—and she returned to the States with Hughes.
After a summer on Cape Cod, the two poets settled in
Northampton and Plath took up her appointment as an
instructor in English at her alma mater, maintaining her
strict schedule of studying, reading, and writing poetry.
Her goal, she wrote, was to be "The Poetess of America
(as Ted will be The Poet of England and her domin-
ions)."

Plath and Hughes returned to England in December
1959, settling at first in London. It was here that their
two children were born: Frieda Rebecca in April 1960,
and Nicholas Farrar in January 1962. Up to their return
to England, Plath had been successful in placing poems
in the leading periodicals, but suffered repeated rejection
in her attempts to place a first collection. On February
11, 1960, however, she signed a contract with Heine-
mann for *The Colossus,* her first published book of poems,
which appeared in October of that year. (Heinemann
also agreed to publish her then unfinished novel, *The Bell
Jar.*)

In the first two months of 1961 Plath endured a mis-
carriage and an appendectomy; her marriage to Hughes
was also becoming strained. Still she wrote, and wrote,
and wrote, accumulating poems for a planned second col-
lection and continued work on *The Bell Jar.* She was
awarded a 1961 Eugene F. Saxton Fellowship to assist
her in the completion of her novel. And she was the edi-
tor of *American Poetry Now,* a supplement to Oxford Uni-

versity Press's *Critical Quarterly*. Plath was pregnant again, in the summer of 1961, when the family moved to Devon.

In March of 1962 the BBC broadcast, as a radio play, Plath's "Three Women: A Monologue for Three Voices." Hughes later identified this poem as "a bridge between *The Colossus* and *Ariel*, both in the change of style from the first half to the last and in that it was written to be read aloud." By June, in addition to working on *The Bell Jar*, Plath had begun the poems that eventually appeared in *Ariel*. During that summer, her relationship with Hughes worsened. After a brief vacation in Ireland, the couple decided to separate; and Plath moved back to London and immersed herself in caring for her children, finally completing her novel, and writing poems at an increasingly breathtaking pace. A few days before Christmas 1962, she moved with the children into a London flat once occupied by William Butler Yeats.

In early January 1963, *The Bell Jar* was at last published, under the pseudonym of Victoria Lucas, after considerable hesitation on Plath's part: She was concerned, on the one hand, that her mother and others might be hurt by it and, on the other hand, that it might lessen her hard-won stature as a poet. (The novel would be republished under its author's actual name, by Faber, in 1965 and by Harper & Row in the United States, in 1971.) By this time, Plath was in desperate circumstances. Her marriage was effectively over, she and the children were ill, the winter was the coldest in a century, and her money was running out. But she was still writing, more furiously than ever, rising very early in the morning and completing as many as five poems in a week, sometimes as many as three in a single day. And she had begun a second novel, *Double Exposure,* the 130 manuscript pages of which have apparently been lost. During just the five weeks before her death she completed twelve poems, all of which were to be included in *Ariel.*

Early on the morning of February 11, 1963, after setting out the children's breakfast and leaving a note for the babysitter, Plath turned on the cooking gas and killed herself. She was buried in Heptonstall, Yorkshire, England.

At the time of her death, Plath was already becoming something of a legend; and there were immediate demands that her post-*Colossus* poems be published in book form. Most of the poems that have since established her lasting reputation appeared, in fact, only after her death. The process, with Ted Hughes acting as compiler and editor, began with *Ariel* in 1965, one of the most celebrated volumes of poetry of this century.

Most of the poems included in the final Hughes-edited *Ariel* were written during the latter months of 1962 and January and February of 1963. In the final six weeks of her life, Plath completed thirteen poems. Hughes selected nine of these final poems for inclusion in *Ariel,* as well as five earlier poems ("Mary's Song," "The Hanging Man," "Little Fugue," "Years," and "Poppies in July") that Plath herself had not included in her manuscript version of the collection. Conversely, he eliminated twelve poems that were among the forty-one left by Plath in her manuscript binder. However, the *Ariel* poems that would bring the greatest acclaim and provoke the most controversy were included in both versions of the manuscript. These include "Lady Lazarus," "Tulips," "Ariel," "Medusa," "Fever 103°," and—perhaps the most renowned of all—"Daddy." "I am writing the best poems of my life," Plath wrote to her mother in late 1962, a few months before her death. "They will make my name."

The year 1965 also saw the appearance of the limited-edition *Uncollected Poems* (London: Turret Books), containing ten late poems. In 1967 the May issue of the *Harvard Advocate* printed a collection of "Early Poems," and two years later the *Times Literary Supplement* printed fifty of Plath's early unpublished poems. London's Sceptre Press brought out the limited-edition *Wreath for a Bridal* in 1970. This was followed, in 1971, in both Britain and the United States, by *Crossing the Water: Transitional Poems,* which collected poems written between the autumn of 1960 and late 1961, as well as nine poems that had been included in the British edition of *The Colossus* but not in the American edition. According to Ted Hughes's editorial note, the poems in *Winter Trees* (Britain, 1971; U.S., 1972)—which completed the separate-volume series of Plath's poems—"are all out of the batch from which the *Ariel* poems were more or less arbitrarily chosen and they were all composed in the last year of Sylvia Plath's life."

The Collected Poems—published in 1981, again edited and annotated by Hughes—brings together all of Plath's mature poetry, published and unpublished and including a selection of fifty early poems, from "Bitter Strawberries" (the 1950 poem published in *The Christian Science Monitor*) through "Edge" and the other poems completed during her final week. It received the 1982 Pulitzer Prize for Poetry.

Author biography
by Hal Hager

Books by Sylvia Plath

HarperPerennial

ARIEL

Widely considered her masterpiece, these are Sylvia Plath's final, shattering poems, which dazzle with their lyricism, their surprising vivid imagery, and their wit.
"In these poems . . . Sylvia Plath becomes herself, becomes something imaginary, newly, wildly, and subtly created." —Robert Lowell
ISBN 0-06-093172-8 (Perennial Classic paperback)

THE BELL JAR

Sylvia Plath's only novel, this is the classic, semi-autobiographical account of one woman's downward spiral into depression and madness. Also available from Caedmon Audio, performed by Academy Award–winning actress Frances McDormand.
"Witty and disturbing. . . . [This] is not a potboiler, nor a series of ungrateful caricatures; it is literature." —*New York Times*
ISBN 0-06-017490-0 (HarperCollins hardcover)
ISBN 0-06-093018-7 (Perennial Classic paperback)
ISBN 0-694-51730-5 (audiocassette)

THE COLLECTED POEMS

Containing all of the poems that Sylvia Plath wrote after 1956, *The Collected Poems* won the Pulitzer Prize for poetry and was edited, annotated, and has an introduction by Ted Hughes.
"The aim of the present complete edition . . . [is] to set everything in as true a chronological order as is possible, so that the whole progress and achievement of this unusual poet will become accessible to readers." —Ted Hughes
ISBN 0-06-090900-5 (paperback)

CROSSING THE WATER

The powerful and haunting "transitional poems" of Sylvia Plath, written just prior to her most celebrated work, *Ariel*.
ISBN 0-06-090789-4 (paperback)

LETTERS HOME

A collection of correspondence from 1950 to 1963, spanning the time between Plath's first letter as a freshman at Smith to one sent only a week before her death.
ISBN 0-06-097491-5 (paperback)

JOHNNY PANIC AND THE BIBLE OF DREAMS

Now available for the first time in more than ten years, this stunning collection of Sylvia Plath's best short stories, prose, and diary excerpts showcases the writer's genius.
ISBN 0-06-095529-5 (paperback)

SYLVIA PLATH READS

This compelling audiocassette features Sylvia Plath's classic readings of some of her most famous poems, including "Leaving Early," "Candles," and "Disquieting Muses."
ISBN 1-55994-570-2 (HarperAudio audiocassette)

Available at bookstores everywhere, or call 1-800-331-3761 to order.